HORRORS OF THE NIGHT

Part 3

A Collection of Short Stories

TOM COLEMAN

HORRORS OF THE NIGHT
Part 3

TOM COLEMAN

Copyright

This is a work of fiction. Names, characters, places, and incidents either are products of the author's imagination or are used fictitiously. Any similarity to actual events or locales or persons, living or dead, is entirely coincidental.

Copyright © 2021 [Tom Coleman] – All Rights Reserved

All rights reserved. No part of this publication may be reproduced, stored in or introduced into a retrieval system, or transmitted, in any form, or by any means (electronic, mechanical, photocopying, recording, or otherwise) without the prior written permission of the copyright owner. The author acknowledges the trademarked status and trademark owners of various products referenced status and trademark owners of various products referenced in this work of fiction, which have been used without permission. The publication / use of the trademarks is not authorized, associated with or sponsored by the trademark owners.

Horrors of the Night 3
BN Publishing
ISBN 978-4-3568-1682-9

ABOUT THE AUTHOR

"This book is horror redefined. Dark and with more twists than a labyrinth. I look forward to reading more from this author."
Amazon reader about Horrors Next Door collection

Since he was a child, he shared a great interest in riddles, mystery and the abnormal. He loved the thrill of having his mind puzzled and astonished by an enigma.

Today, he writes books for people who share his enthusiasm for scary and mystifying stories. If you love horror mystery you will love his books.

We are gathering all people with a passion for Horror/Mystery/Thrillers in our special group. If you want to be in and connect with us, join our group :)

Join here:

https://www.facebook.com/groups/541739063097831/

TABLE OF CONTENTS

HORRORS OF THE NIGHT Part 3 3
ABOUT THE AUTHOR 5
THE OTHER SIDE 9
    Chapter 1 11
    Chapter 2 27
    Chapter 3 43
    Chapter 4 61
    Chapter 5 77
    Chapter 6 87
THE CURSE OF HERNANDEZ PART THREE 113
    CHAPTER FIVE: Pain 115
    CHAPTER FOUR: I can't believe this 135
HONEST REVIEW REQUEST 155

HORRORS OF THE NIGHT

8

TOM COLEMAN

HORRORS OF THE NIGHT

THE OTHER SIDE

9

TOM COLEMAN

HORRORS OF THE NIGHT

10

TOM COLEMAN

Chapter 1

"It is my great pride to give you the graduates of Carlton Boarding High," said Principal Coleman with a smile. The tall, grey-haired principal stood back as the hall filled with the deafening sound of celebration. Parents, friends, students, staff members, and school visitors clapped and cheered in unison as the youngsters trooped onto the podium in the school's hall. This was it--the moment Joe Phillips had dreamed of since he'd started Carlton Boarding High.

Joe scanned the crowd, grinning from ear to ear. His little sister jumped excitedly where she stood. His mom and dad had their hands busy with applause. Mom was teary-eyed and flashing a tooth-glistening smile. Dad, on the other hand, wore a small smile.

"Thank you," Joe said under his breath.

HORRORS OF THE NIGHT

His father nodded amidst the unending applause as though he'd heard his near-silent words of gratitude.

Joe would have continued staring at his family through the rest of the graduation program had his best friend, Kyle, not pulled him by the neck.

"This is it, bro," he said into Joe's ear. His voice was raised so Joe could hear him. Kyle took off his graduation cap and waited for the signal.

Realizing what he'd nearly missed, Joe hurriedly removed his graduation cap just in time to throw it into the air alongside his mates. It was official: they were finally high school graduates.

***

The rest of the graduation ceremony was a breeze of teary-eyed goodbyes, the exchange of numbers, and loads of promises to keep in touch. It was how things were supposed to be, and Joe enjoyed every moment of it.

After a few more moments of excitement, Joe was in his family's minivan. Dad was driving, and that meant his mom had the four hours' drive time to herself. There was no better way for her to spend the four hours save chatting excitedly with her son about his graduation and probably chip in one or two hints about college. That was her trademark. She wasn't as reserved as her husband. Although Joe was tired from the ceremony, he didn't mind the chitchat.

"So, I spoke to--"

"Come on, Liz, let the boy rest. You've been going on for the last two hours," Mr. Phillips said, finally. They were his first words since the journey had begun.

"But hon--" his wife began to protest.

"No buts, Liz. I'm sure Joe's had more than enough talk for today. Let the young man rest his head and dream about his friends," Mr. Phillips said, cutting off his wife. "Am I right, Joe?" He glanced at his son via the rearview mirror.

Joe gave him a weak smile in response. While he didn't want to hurt his mom's feelings, he definitely needed to rest his head.

"Oh," Liz started, her voice low, "guess you should rest your head now, dear." Joe's mom adjusted herself in her seat and remained quiet.

Joe stared for a while, wondering whether to spark another conversation with his mom. He knew she'd been hurt by being told to keep quiet, no matter how little. He hadn't liked that bit, even though he knew that his dad meant well, and he desperately needed to rest his head. Jeanne, his little sister, was fast asleep with her head on his shoulder-- sleeping was hardly a problem for a ten-year-old.

"Guess I'll be joining Jeanne, then," he said under his breath. He adjusted himself, snuggling into the seat, and allowing his eyes to drift shut. No sooner had he done this than he was off to sleep and faster than he'd expected.

***

"Well, well--look who's finished high school," said a voice much like Joe's.

"Huh? What?" Joe muttered. His eyelids fluttered.

"Oh, no, you don't," the voice said.

Joe felt a breeze brush over his eyes, and his eyelids felt like lead. "Who's there?" Joe asked, turning his face from side to side. Try as hard as he could he could not open his eyes.

"Relax, Joe, " the voice said again.

Joe's head was forced to a standstill. Dread filled him as he wondered where he was and who was holding him captive. He couldn't feel anything touching him, yet he was heavily restrained.

"I'm a friend, Joe. I just came to give my hearty congratulations," the voice said after a moment of silence. "You don't know me, but I know you, Joe. I know everything about you.

"Let's just say that I'm that friend who's always been there, but you never really cared to know," it said. "I figured that if I'd said congratulations while you were busy with your other friends, you'd hardly hear me, so I decided to wait, at least until I knew we were alone and you'd hear me.

"Anyway, congratulations, Joe. I hope you had fun," the voice said. "Not to be a bother or anything, but I'm here fo you. You and I are going to have so much fun soon." It chuckled.

A few minutes passed. Joe slowly felt himself regain control of his body. He felt as if the environment around him was slowing down. Once he could control his eyelids, Joe opened his eyes and jerked upright.

"Wow, easy there, mister, " Mr. Phillips said to his son, who had nearly jumped out of his seat.

"We just got home," he said.

"Oh, okay," Joe said. He took in a loud breath, rubbed his eyes, and looked at his mom, whose brows were frowned; she looked concerned.

"It's nothing, Mom. I just had a weird dream, that's all," Joe said, stretching slightly. Although something didn't feel right about what he'd experienced, it was better not to give Mom something else to worry about. He knew how overprotective she could be when there was something to worry about, and he didn't want that kind of attention, besides. At least, not at that moment.

"Hmm. Guess you're starting to miss your friends back at school," Mr. Phillips said.

Joe smiled slightly as if to say, "Maybe."

"Anyway, you only just left them four hours ago. I'm sure you'll be just fine after a week or two. Didn't you get a few cards and phone numbers?" Mr. Phillips queried with an arched brow.

Joe nodded and mumbled something along the lines of, "I guess I could place a few calls."

"It's settled, then, " Mr. Phillips said, getting out of his side of the minivan. "Come--help me with some of the stuff in the trunk."

"But John, " Liz protested, stepping out of the minivan.

"Don't worry, mom. I'm fully rested. I can take the stuff out of the trunk," Joe offered, and he stepped out of the car, as well.

"No, you can't," Liz said sharply. Her eyes did not leave her husband, who was trying to stifle his laughter. "It's your big day today, and I intend for you to enjoy it fully," she added, her voice turning sweet.

"Come on, Mom. Taking some of my stuff out of the trunk won't make a difference. It's just normal stuff," Joe said with a shrug.

"Jeanne?" she called.

Her daughter, who'd been watching her family from inside the minivan, peeked out her head.

"Come with me. Let's leave the men to do their thing," she said sweetly.

"Okay, Mom," Jeanne replied, and she made her way promptly out of the minivan, skipped a little, took her mom's outstretched hand, and walked in-step with her.

"I'm sure you agree that I'm right, " Liz said to her daughter as they made their way into the house. They lived in a quiet neighborhood with rows of houses on either side of the road. Each house had a neatly mowed lawn secured with a low fence. It was the perfect setup for mild chitchats with the neighbors, but at that moment, none of the neighbors were in sight. It was just them, having arrived a little past five pm without fanfare or inquiries from nosey neighbors.

HORRORS OF THE NIGHT

***

The kitchen and dining arrangements were Liz's turf, and she did exactly as she pleased. First, it started by banning Joe and his father from the kitchen while she sorted out dinner preparations. By the time she was out of the kitchen and had set the round dining table, there were two steaming bowls sitting in the middle of the dining table, one with spaghetti and another with chicken. A third bowl held mouthwatering salad.

Mr. Phillips whistled when he saw the dished laid out before him. "Now, this is the real celebration," he said, smacking his lips.

The first bit of the feast went without a hassle until Mr. Phillips decided to help himself to more.

Liz acted fast, her fork intercepting that of her husband just before he could pick up a piece of chicken. "The latest graduates get to pick first," she said with a wink.

Her husband stared. When he recovered himself, Mr. Phillips tried outsmarting his wife by pretending to remove his fork, but she was ready for him. No sooner had he tried to sink his fork back into the bowl than she was there to intercept it.

"Come on, Liz," Mr. Phillips whined. "He's not even done with his plate."

"Oh, well. Guess we'll have to wait for him, then," his wife replied sweetly, her fork still deflecting that of her husband's.

Joe looked at his parents, who were hunched over the dining table in a battle of forks. It was as silly as it was endearing. This was the part about home he'd missed terribly while he'd been in school. It wasn't as though school was all that bad, but it definitely didn't compare to home.

Joe's mind flooded with loving memories of the past, and a streak of tears fell down his cheek. It was enough to break the battle between his mom and dad, who turned to look at him. "I... I love you guys," Joe said with a shaky voice.

Mr. Phillips stretched a hand to Joe and rubbed his head.

His wife ambled over to her son and buried him in a hug.

"We love you, too, son," Mr. Phillips said in response. "I am proud of you," he added.

Jeanne had quietly joined in the hug alongside her mom.

For a while, it seemed as though dinner might end with the hug. But Mr. Phillips saw his chance, went for the bowl of chicken, and took off with it.

"John," his wife screamed. She broke the hug to chase after him.

Mr. Phillips laughed as he evaded his wife, and Joe and his little sister joined in. It was, indeed, one of those days.

***

The night wore on smoothly, and it was finally time for Joe to retire. With all the excitement he'd had, his body needed all the rest it could get.

HORRORS OF THE NIGHT

Joe slumped onto his bed and gave a sigh of relief. It had been a great day. Memories of his friends at school came rushing in, and he took his time savoring each one. The pranks, the tests, the difficult times, the games, the hangouts... he replayed every moment dear to him. Kyle, his best friend, had pulled through on many occasions for him, and it was with a mix of regret that he realized it was all over. At least, their high school years were over, and the likelihood of going to the same college was bleak.

Just then, it hit him: he hadn't called any of his friends, especially not Kyle, whom he'd promised to call once he arrived home.

"Well, then, let's see what he's up to," he muttered. Joe turned over on his side and slid his hands over to his bedside dresser, where his phone laid on the edge, switched off.

He picked up his phone, switched it on, and waited for the phone to complete its booting process. Not too long after it was done booting, a string of notifications sounded. Text messages. Not just from Kyle but from a ton of others.

"Guess I'm a little late," he said with a smirk, and he opened the first message from Kyle.

It read: "Hey, man--how's home? Nothing out of the ordinary happening here. A few words from my old man and that's all. PS, the gang's hanging out next Saturday. I'll send the details later."

Joe smiled, and his mind drifted to what Kyle had said concerning his dad. It was always a few words that were said between them. He was the only son of a single father, and his dad never joked about Kyle's career path. For what it was worth, his dad had plans to get him into one of the top colleges. His dad was unlike Joe's, who had a good sense of humor despite being reserved. While a good sense of humor could calm some tense moments, it wasn't always enough. Bills still had to be paid, and Joe knew how much he had to work to earn a scholarship to ease the burden on his parents. It had paid off with a partial scholarship, but the depressing thought of why things weren't better than they currently were always hung out in the back of his mind.

"No time for that now," Joe muttered, shaking himself out of his thoughts. He needed to call Kyle.

Joe switched to his dialer, flexed his finger over his phone's screen, and tapped out the number off the top of his head. Without crosschecking that he'd dialed correctly, he hit the dial button and brought the phone to his ear.

For a moment, there was no ring, which prompted Joe to check his phone. The silence was odd. Joe checked his phone, puzzled at the silly mistake he'd made: he'd unconsciously dialed his own phone number. That explained why there was no ring; it couldn't connect.

He smiled lazily and moved his finger toward the red button to disconnect. In the few seconds it took for his finger to press the red button, the call connected.

"Hello, Joe," an eerily familiar voice said.

HORRORS OF THE NIGHT

26

TOM COLEMAN

Chapter 2

"H-hello?" Joe stuttered. "Who is this?"

"Ha-ha--don't you know already?" the speaker asked. There was an unsettling feeling in those words.

"What? I don't know you," Joe said, steeling his voice, so it didn't sound frightened. The other speaker sounded all too familiar to ignore, and it made his skin crawl.

"Come on, Joe--don't tell me you've forgotten so quickly. Or didn't I make that much of an impression the first time?" the voice retorted.

"Look," Joe said firmly, "whatever game this is, I don't want any part in it. I don't know you, and I don't know what kind of hack got you into my phone number."

"Oh, strong words, " the voice said with a chuckle. "Maybe I should cut to the chase then."

"Yes, quit stalling and answer my question," Joe demanded, his initial fear turning to a mild annoyance. He was much too tired to continue the conversation with the strange voice on the other end of the call.

Silence reigned between the duo for what felt like hours. Joe, who couldn't take it anymore, sighed and was about to hang up when the voice spoke once more.

"I am you, Joe Phillips," it said.

A chill ran down Joe's spine at the words. Despite his room being mildly warm, he felt eerily cold. There was something about that voice that screamed terror. "Ex-excuse me?" Joe finally said, but there was no response. "He-hello?" Joe queried after a few seconds passed in silence, but there was still no response.

He drew his phone away from his ear and glanced at the screen. The call timer blinked steadily, displaying "00:00."

HORRORS OF THE NIGHT

"That's not possible," Joe muttered, feeling confused by the display on his phone's screen. Just then, the call dropped.

Joe stared at his phone. The screen had long turned off due to inactivity. His tired mind reeled with unease. He'd heard of people dialing their own phone numbers for fun, but he'd never heard of calls like that going through. It was odd that his had gone through, not to mention the creepy turn it had taken when the person on the other end had claimed to be him. As much as he wanted to write it off as a prankster who had hacked into his phone number, there was something about it that made him shiver. He'd heard that voice before. It was the same voice as he'd heard in his dream when he'd taken a short nap on the way home.

Unsure as to what to do, Joe double-tapped on the screen of his phone. It came on, and as expected, his number was the first on the call log. He stared, his finger too hesitant to redial. He didn't feel so sleepy anymore.

Joe steeled himself, closed his eyes, and let his finger drift to the redial button. A few minutes passed in silence, prompting Joe to take a peek at his phone screen. No sooner did he do this than the screen lit up with the call timer, which read "00:00."

"H-hello?" Joe stuttered

"Hello, Joe. Guess you finally decided to call again," the voice replied.

Joe gulped. "Tell me again: who are you?" he asked, trying to maintain as much control over his voice as possible. To an observer, it would seem as if he were having a normal conversation, but on the inside, he was shaking.

"I am you, Joe," the voice said.

"But that doesn't make any sense," Joe responded.

The voice chuckled and said, "Maybe. Aren't you the owner of this phone number?"

Joe replied in the affirmative.

"Since you're the owner, aren't you supposed to be the one who receives calls on this number?" it queried.

"Yes, but that's not the point," Joe retorted. "I am the owner, and I am the one to receive the calls. I am me," he said, his voice rising.

"Yes. I agree, " the voice said flatly.

"Y-you do?" Joe was taken aback by the response.

"Yes, indeed, Joe. You're you... and I am you," the voice said

"But how? It's not possible that when I call my line, I answer my own call to my own line, if that makes any sense at all," Joe said. His frustration was starting to show.

"Ha-ha. Don't think too deeply on this, Joe." The voice chuckled.

Joe grumbled. "if you claim to be me, then you must know what I know--"

"Like what you like, and hate what you hate?" the voice said, completing Joe's line of thought.

"Wait--how did you?" Joe asked in disbelief. He hadn't expected the voice to steal into his thoughts and complete his sentence.

"Guess that helps convince you a little, doesn't it?" The voice chuckled.

"You know, it's already late, " Joe started, "Mom and Dad are probably asleep--"

"That's not what's on your mind, is it Joe?" the voice retorted.

Joe kept quiet, fishing desperately for an answer in his head.

"Kyle is fine, and he isn't all that bothered about you not calling," it added.

"Shit," Joe exclaimed. He'd been fishing in his head for an excuse to end the call, and the voice had picked up on it.

HORRORS OF THE NIGHT

"I understand this is a little confusing for you, Joe, but it is what it is; I am you," it said.

Unsure of what to say, Joe kept quiet. The voice didn't seem to mind the silence. The duo remained like that until Joe felt himself drift off to sleep.

"You know, it's not exactly smart to sleep while on the phone," the voice said.

Joe's eyes shot open. His phone was still by his ear, but the statement hadn't come from his phone--he'd heard it in his head.

Alarmed, he tapped the red button on his phone's screen to end the call but nothing happened. The call timer kept blinking, meaning he was still on the call. He tried a few more frustrated taps, but Joe couldn't get the call to end.

"You know, instead of trying to run, how about you ask me all you want to know?" the voice said amidst Joe's incessant tapping. That got a reaction from Joe, who paused as though considering the offer. Creepy as it was, Joe needed to know who he was dealing

HORRORS OF THE NIGHT

with. First, it seemed like he was dealing with a top-notch hacker, but that didn't explain how the voice was able to enter his head.

"Fine," Joe said finally. His shoulders dropped in an unconscious shrug. "Since you don't plan on letting me off the call, tell me who you are again?"

"We've already gone through this, Joe: I am you. Your other half, the part that exists between here and there," it retorted.

"What does that me--"

"It's not yet time for you to know that," the voice said, its tone dark and foreboding.

"Oh," Joe said. "So, how does this you being me work?"

"Well, I know all about you. I was there at each point of memory," the voice replied. "I can help you recall any memory, and I can pretty much help you get into someone else's mind," it added.

The latter comment caught Joe's attention, but just as he was about to ask for clarification, the voice took his cue and said, "Yes, I can share your thoughts with another. Make said person see and hear thoughts as though you're speaking to them directly."

"Wait--are you saying that you can connect me telepathically to another person? Like read and talk to minds?" Joe asked, his interest piqued.

"Well, if that's how you understand it, then yes," the voice replied.

"Wow," Joe said. There was nothing more he could think of to utter.

"But wait--how, exactly, are you able to do that?" he asked after a while.

"Let's just say I am your un-tethered self. Your other side," it replied.

"Hmm," Joe muttered as his mind processed what he'd heard.

"Just so you know, you're not the first," the voice quipped. "There have been others before you, and there are others like you."

HORRORS OF THE NIGHT

"You mean there are others who can call their phone lines and link to strange voices that claim to be them and talk about stuff that's never been heard before?" Joe retorted. This didn't seem to sit well with the voice, who kept quiet at his remark.

"Hello?" Joe called, but there was no response. After waiting a few minutes without a response, Joe tried disconnecting the call once more.

"Careful, Joe, you may hurt yourself," the voice finally said. At this, the call dropped by itself, leaving Joe staring uneasily at his phone's screen.

It had been a crazy night for Joe, who had kept going back and forth between being creeped out and intrigued. The talk about mind reading had piqued his interest, and he'd already thought of a few people he'd like to try it on, but his mind had also been thrown into unease at the last words he'd heard, which were foreboding.

Joe sighed heavily, dropped his phone on his bedside table, and got comfortable in the bed. His mind was intrigued, confused, and scared at the same time. He just couldn't understand how something could be both creepy and fascinating. For what it was worth, he was done for the day, and he could finally rest.

***

"Please, don't do this--please," Joe pleaded desperately, clambering for the support of the wall behind him. Five lanky figures loomed over him, their faces obscured by darkness. He was cornered.

"You know what time it is, Joe?" one of the figures queried. A pale hand dropped heavily onto his shoulder. The weight forced him harshly to the ground. There was a splash as Joe fell to the water-laden tile floor. He was locked in the bathroom. Worse off, it was flooded.

"It's teatime," the same figure said and burst out laughing. The five lanky frames shook eerily as they burst into maniacal bouts of laughter.

"Please! I'll do what you asked. I'll fix your notes... homework... anything," Joe cried.

"Too late, little man. First, you drink, then you fix our mistakes," the lead figure said. In a swift motion, Joe felt himself being hoisted onto his feet by two powerful hands. The force with which they'd lifted him sent him crashing into the wall. He grunted as pain shot through his body; screaming was futile.

Without giving him a moment's breath, he was lifted high into the air. Four pairs of arms held him firmly on both arms and legs, so firmly he had very little wiggle-room.

The chant of "Teatime" continued as they dragged him through the flooded bathroom passage. A stall at the far end of the passage gleamed an ominous shade of red. That was his judgment room, and he knew what was coming.

A kick sent the door of the stall flying open. Almost immediately, he was thrown to the floor, his head barely missing the decrepit ceramic toilet tank.

Joe raised a weak palm to his nose as the stench from the toilet slammed heavily into his nostrils. Not that it mattered, though. It was only a matter of seconds before he would be in the toilet, head first.

"Not so tough now, are you?" one of the figures queried Joe as he was yanked to his feet.

With his eyes shut, Joe gulped as he felt himself being raised by his legs. In a matter of seconds, he was dangling above the toilet. In the last moments before he was dropped into it, Joe felt himself recoil. Something had stirred in him. Was it disgust at his weakness? Hatred for his oppressors?

Just then, he heard, "All this time, Joe, you've ignored me."

~~~

Joe jerked out of his sleep, panting and sweating. He darted his eyes from left to right, glancing around his darkened room. It was an act designed to reassure him that he was safe, that all he'd seen and all he'd felt had been nothing but a dream.

He heaved a sigh but remained seated in the dark, and his eyes began to play tricks on him. The shadows seemed to move in the periphery of his vision, but each time he turned to look, nothing was there.

"Not tonight," he said under his breath, and he reached for his phone. There was a wave of peace when he switched on the phone's torch app, which he used to scan around the room to make sure there were no figures hidden in the corners. Once he was satisfied he was alone, he dragged himself off the bed and walked groggily out of his room.

Joe made his way to the fridge in the kitchen and pulled out a can of soda. He downed the entire contents in a single gulp, wiped his mouth with the back of his hand, and sighed. It wasn't the first time he'd had that nightmare. As a matter of fact, it was one of five recurring nightmares, and at the end of each one, he heard the same voice saying the same words.

He tossed the can into the recycling bin by the kitchen door and went off toward his room, but just as he got to his door, he made a U-turn. He definitely wasn't going to get any more sleep after the nightmare, so there was no point lying in the darkness in which his mind would only unleash a new chapter of unease.

Joe retraced his steps, went into the living room, picked up the TV remote, and sank into the sofa. After a few clicks, he found a channel airing a documentary on animals. He glanced at his phone's screen. The time read one o'clock am.

"Guess I won't fall asleep till a little past two, then," he muttered to himself and dropped the phone beside him.

Watching TV so late at night turned out to be the best option for Joe because he didn't realize when he'd dozed off. It wasn't until the TV suddenly blared static that he jerked up from the sofa and blinked to settle his eyes to the environment.

He sighed, went groggily to the TV, and switched it off. He rubbed his eyes and stared at the dark screen for a while. After a few minutes passed with him standing and staring, he sighed once more and turned to go to his room, but as he did, he heard some movement outside. Someone was out on the lawn.

Chapter 3

Joe's nerves twitched as he listened. The hairs on his arms stood on end, and he couldn't help the sudden chill around him. There was someone on the lawn.

Unsure of what to do, Joe crept quietly into the living room. He wasn't a fighter, so there was no way he could exchange blows with a home intruder. At best, he could keep his hands firmly on the door to resist it being forced open.

Standing in front of the door, Joe peered through the door's peephole. While the view wasn't great at night, it would help him catch a glimpse of the intruder. It was pitch-black outside, save the flickering overhead bulb on the porch. Its shine hardly cast a few inches down on the lawn.

The footsteps grew a little louder as Joe peered through the peephole. He could hardly see, but the sound of footsteps told him the intruder was approaching the main entrance. Joe swallowed, took his gaze from the peephole, and glanced around, looking for a weapon—anything he could use at all—but there was nothing. Resigned, he gulped and took another peek out.

Joe jerked back from the peephole, nearly tumbling backward as he did.

A lone figure had appeared on the porch, its head bowed in the flickering light. Panic had set in fully, and Joe was about to take flight to his room. Just then, he paused and turned back to the peephole. Something seemed familiar about the figure standing on the porch.

Joe was hesitant, but he steeled himself and took another peek. Just then, a wave of shock and relief washed through him—the figure had on clothes he'd seen on several nights at home: Jeanne's pajamas. He had the presence of mind to wonder what she was doing out in the dark, and then he got his answer.

HORRORS OF THE NIGHT

The figure stirred, lifted its head slightly, and revealed a placid face, its eyes shut.

"Jeanne?" Joe said once he'd recognized the face. He grumbled, scolding himself for being afraid. Jeanne was a sleepwalker. He should have known she was likely to have an episode.

Relieved he wasn't dealing with an intruder, Joe opened the door and stepped onto the porch. It was chilly outside.

He took Jeanne by the hand, led her in, and shut the door quickly behind them. There was an unsettling feeling in the pit of his stomach that wasn't really about the chill outside.

Jeanne was still fast asleep despite being on her feet.

A little smile crept on his face as he watched his little sister sleep without a care as to what might happen to her. He let out a sigh and lifted his sister into his arms, cradling her like a baby. With her head resting against his shoulder, he took off toward her room, careful not to make any sudden moves that might disturb her sleep.

Jeanne hardly stirred on the trip from the living room to her room. It wasn't until Joe had placed her in her bed and covered her with a blanket that she stirred to snuggle into the bed for warmth.

Joe smiled at the sight and left her room quietly. Not only did he shut the door quietly, but he locked her in.

He reflected that Jeanne's sleepwalking episode was nothing special for him, and he went back to the living room and dropped back onto the sofa as his phone chimed with a message notification.

"Good job, big bro," the text said.

As simple as it sounded, Joe's sleepy eyes glared widely at the message. The unsettling feeling in his gut increased when he took note of the sender to see that it had come from his own phone number.

Angry yet uneasy, Joe turned off his phone and willed for sleep to take him. He was better off sleeping on the sofa than having to put up with the shadowy corners of his room.

***

Joe's eyes twitched when the sun's rays persisted, intruding on his sleep. He grumbled, and his eyes opened slowly to stare directly above him. Joe blinked, his eyes darting around, taking note of his environment. He remembered sleeping it off on the sofa, yet there he was, in his room. He shrugged it off, reasoning that his mom or dad had probably had a hand in it.

"Morning, Mom," Joe greeted his mom, who was fixing breakfast when he walked into the kitchen. She was focused on the eggs she was frying. A plate of toast sat on the kitchen counter, and Joe reached for a slice.

He took a bite and asked, "Mom, did you help me to my room last night?"

His mom didn't take her eyes off the eggs while replying.

"No, honey. I didn't step out of my room last night. Why—did something happen?"

Joe shook his head. He watched his mother in silence as she continued preparing breakfast—toast and eggs hit the spot—and he had a flash of the night before: the conversation with the strange voice, Jeanne's episode, the nightmare, and him waking up in bed. Joe shook his head, shut his eyes tightly, and willed the images away.

"Are you all right?" came his father's voice.

Joe opened his eyes and looked at his dad, confused.

His father nodded at Joe's hands, which were gripping the side of the table firmly.

Joe got the message and loosened his grip.

"Yeah, I'm fine. Just had a little flash, that's all."

HORRORS OF THE NIGHT

"You slept well?" his dad queried, to which Joe nodded. His hands twitched, but he clasped them quickly together.

Joe asked his dad about the night before, but his dad shrugged in response. Just then, Jeanne stepped into the kitchen, rubbing her eyes; she'd just woken up.

"Well, the sleeper's finally awake," Joe said. He laughed.

Jeanne looked blankly at him and turned to her dad.

"You were sleepwalking last night, little one, and I helped you to your room, remember?" Joe said.

"No, I don't think I walked last night," Jeanne replied with a little pout.

"Oh yeah? Then how come I carried you back to your room like a baby and locked the door?"

"Daddy, Joe's mocking me," Jeanne whined, pulling at their dad's trousers.

HORRORS OF THE NIGHT

Joe laughed and recounted the episode to their parents, but in the end, neither Mom nor Dad was laughing.

"Am I missing something?" Joe asked, looking from his mom to his dad.

Jeanne didn't find it funny either. She kept protesting that she hadn't sleepwalked the night before.

"Are you sure you slept well, Joe?" his dad queried with a raised brow.

"Jeanne hasn't sleepwalked for about three months now. It's why we no longer lock her door at night," his mom added.

Joe was perplexed. If his little sister no longer sleepwalked, then who had he seen outside the night before? Worse, who had he brought into the house and placed in the same room as his sister?

He darted out of the kitchen and hurried straight to Jeanne's room. His dad went after him.

HORRORS OF THE NIGHT

Joe threw the blanket off frantically, crouched low, and checked beneath the bed, but there was nothing out of the ordinary.

"Whoa, whoa, whoa—slow down, young man," his dad said, but Joe was past hearing as he upturned Jeanne's boxes and ransacked her closet.

His dad stood there as if too dumbstruck to act.

***

It was silent inside the minivan. Joe – their son stared out through the window for most of the drive. Nobody said anything, not even Liz - his mom, who seemed greatly discomfited by the silence. Whatever had happened at home, they had all settled on an unspoken agreement to say nothing, at least until Joe decided to.

Mr. and Mrs. Phillips knew their son dealt with depression that tended toward manic bursts. They knew the bullying he experienced at school didn't help matters, but they had no real options when it came to changing schools. Joe had promised he would be fine, and for a while, he seemed to have kept his promise. His brief holidays hardly experienced incidents of mania or silent depression, but they always saw the sorrow masked in Joe's smile when he was to return to school. Thought they called as often as they could, they couldn't really tell if he was, indeed, doing fine in school.

Now, two years since his last outburst, Joe had had another episode. From recounting an old memory of his sister sleepwalking to making a sudden dash for his sister's room, an old fear had been rekindled.

Whenever Joe drifted into silence, there was no telling when or what would get him back to speaking as lively as he normally did. Since the episode, he hadn't uttered a word, and he hadn't resisted his parents' offer to take a drive to clear his head.

HORRORS OF THE NIGHT

***

"Can I get a new SIM for my phone?" Joe asked quietly. His sudden query after being silent since that morning's episode startled his parents.

"Just feel like changing it since I'm done with school," Joe explained

"Yes... I guess," his mom said uncertainly, looking at her husband for approval. Mr. Phillips nodded without taking his eyes off the road. Whenever Joe was in the throes of one of his bouts, their best option was to give in to his requests. Though the SIM didn't need replacing, it was more about Joe, probably trying to cope.

"Well, we could take you to the service center now, if you don't mind," his mom offered.

Joe shrugged and continued staring out the window. He knew what the others thought about him. His mom, dad, and even some of his neighborhood friends knew about his stained history, but to him, he was pretty much normal, along with his share of life's misgivings.

With what had happened earlier, he knew just who was to blame: the voice that had been messing with him. The calls, the text, and worse off, the intrusions into his mind, had all come from the voice. He'd probably dreamed the whole sleepwalking episode. It was just like one of his post nightmare dreams, where he would wake up from a nightmare, still asleep and dreaming. Whenever such a thing happened, he could hardly separate his dreams from reality until he finally woke up. Just like that morning, he would end up speaking to someone about what seemed to have happened but never did. Kyle knew about these post dream occurrences, and it made it easier for him to clear his head, but his parents were in the dark about it all, and he wasn't keen on telling them just yet.

Talking to his parents about the voice didn't seem like a good idea, either. They'd only freak out and decide it was time to see a therapist, but he didn't want that. Instead, he decided to pretend he was fine. If he spoke and acted as though nothing had happened, they would feel a little relieved, and their relief was his chance to figure things out. For starters, he would block the voice from reaching him.

***

Switching his SIM was pretty easy. Joe made a mental note never to try dialing his own number. He placed a few calls to some friends to inform them about his change of phone number. Kyle was the first he'd called, and the duo spent ample time on the phone, chatting about their plans, particularly the list of fun things they had to do before getting worked up over admission into their respective colleges. As it turned out, Kyle had gotten tickets for them to an after-grad house party, and it was only seven days away.

HORRORS OF THE NIGHT

"Just a minute," Joe said over the phone. He turned to his parents—who were, once more, overshadowed by silence on the drive home—and asked if he could make the trip to the house party slated for the following weekend.

"Well, if it's Kyle, then it shouldn't be a problem," his mom said. His dad nodded in agreement.

Upon receipt of their assent, Joe switched back to Kyle and said, "I'll be there, man."

***

Ever since Joe had changed his SIM, he felt a little more at peace. There had been no voices intruding his mind in weeks, and he relaxed into his environment, checking in with old friends and neighbors. Kyle had come visiting twice, and it had been a blast reliving hilarious memories from their school days.

HORRORS OF THE NIGHT

"Tell me again why you switched your SIM—what happened to the old one?" Kyle asked during one of their conversations.

Joe flinched slightly. "Nothing really, I discovered it was allocated to someone else." Joe said evasively.

"That's odd. You've been using that SIM for a couple of years, and it's all of a sudden allocated to someone else?" Kyle said thoughtfully.

Joe shrugged and said, "Don't look at me—I don't know how it works. I only know that someone else is allocated to my phone number, and I only just discovered it after graduation."

"Oh, well, if you say so. For a moment, it seemed like you wanted to bail on the rest of us." Kyle said jokingly.

Joe scowled and said, "That wouldn't be all that bad. Ha-ha"

The conversation with Kyle dragged on for most of Joe's day until it was time for him to return home, but just as Kyle waved him off after getting into his cab, that old, unsettled feeling crept in once more. While he'd evaded most questions from his friends about the change in phone numbers, Kyle's query had left him uneasy. It reminded him that he hadn't heard the voice in over a month. While disconnecting from the voice had been a relief, he couldn't shake the unease in the pit of his stomach.

"It's nothing. I'm not being traced. There's no one out to get me," Joe reassured himself, shaking off his thoughts of fear.

For every sin, there is a temptation. That was the case with Joe, who couldn't take his eyes off of his phone's screen. It was nighttime, and he dialed out his phone number for the third time that night. He just couldn't shake the feeling of his fingers itching to press the buttons. It was all he could do to resist, by hovering his finger above the dial button. But it was only a matter of time before he went through with it and dialed.

Joe, who kept reminding himself not to press the dial button, found that his fingers no longer yielded to his will. Like an addict falling into a relapse, Joe's thumb finally tapped the dial button, and he shut his eyes.

HORRORS OF THE NIGHT

60

TOM COLEMAN

Chapter 4

"Hello, Joe—how was your little break? I've been waiting for you," the voice responded. The call timer remained steady at 00:00.

At the sound of the eerie voice, Joe pressed the red button in a bid to disconnect the call, but the timer remained active.

The voice chuckled at his futile act. "You should know by now, Joe, that you can't get rid of me. I am you, your untethered self, your other half. We are one and the same, two sides of a coin," it said eerily.

"What do you want? Why are you monitoring me?" Joe asked, his voice heavy with fear and resentment.

"It's really simple, Joe: I want you. I want every bit of you—your life, your bonds, your time, your friends... even your enemies."

HORRORS OF THE NIGHT

"This doesn't make any sense. Why would anyone want—" Joe's protest ended when the voice cut him off.

"There is so much you do not know, Joe. So much you could do, so much I could help you achieve, but here you are, resisting," the voice snapped.

"Be careful, Joe," it said quietly. "I always get what and who I want."

No sooner had the voice uttered these words than the line went dead.

Joe remained seated on his bed, staring at his phone's screen for hours on end. He was genuinely afraid, his body shivering despite the mild room temperature.

That night, time passed slowly for Joe. While the others slept, he stared at the phone until the batterie run out.

***

Drip… drip… drip!

HORRORS OF THE NIGHT

The sound of water drops rang through the empty canvas. It was silent save for the echo of the drops.

"Hello? Anybody here?" Joe heard himself call. It was pitch-black all around him. He felt his way around until he stumbled into a body of water.

He got hurriedly back to his feet. Joe inched slowly forward, feeling as though he was walking deeper into the water. What had previously only covered his ankle had risen to his waist and continued to rise the more he moved forward in the darkness.

"This way," a voice said. There was a strong echo, making it sound ominous.

"A... Are you sure? Is there an exit there? Please, I don't know where I am," Joe pleaded. His eyes darted from left to right, but there was nothing but darkness.

"Over here, Joe. We're waiting, " a much different voice called, carried by the same echo. Though grim, Joe followed the voices, walking deeper into the water that soon threatened to cover his head.

HORRORS OF THE NIGHT

Walking blindly with only echoes as his guide, Joe missed a footing and sunk momentarily into the water around him. Though alarmed, he held his breath and swung his arms desperately around in a bid to reach the surface.

Then came the laughter.

Bubbles floated around Joe, each of them bursting to release the trapped air inside along with the sound of maniacal laughter. Afraid for his life, Joe struggled against the bubbles and insistent pressure preventing him from reaching the surface. Eventually, his will gained dominance, and his head finally bobbed above the water, breathing heavily.

"Had fun?" a voice queried.

Joe blinked, then rubbed his eyes clear. Five shadowy figures stood in an arc around him. He looked up at their faces, and his breath caught in his throat. Pale white faces resembling his glared down at him. Each face had a grin reaching from ear to ear and pitch black eyes. These were his tormentors, and he knew what came after their grin.

"No, no, no... no, please!" Joe screamed as the faces inched closer to his until there was nothing left. It was pitch black.

***

Joe jerked out of his nightmare and flicked his head from side to side. His heart thumped speedily in his chest. His eyes slowly adjusted to the darkness, and he breathed heavily when he realized he was in the safety of his room.

Joe sighed, stepped gingerly out of bed, and took a walk to the bathroom. His intent was simple: wash his face and return to the living room.

He switched on the tap on the bathroom's lone sink, dipped his hand into the pool of water, and shut his eyes. The feel of the water on his skin was soothing.

HORRORS OF THE NIGHT

Joe cupped a little into his hands, splashed the cold water onto his face, and rubbed gently. His eyes stung delightfully and the cold soothed his frayed nerves. Time quietly passed as Joe savored the calm and soothing feeling.

He relaxed and splashed his face again before opening his eyes. Just as he did, his breath nearly left him at the sight before him. Staring back at Joe in the mirror was his own reflection, but rather than his usual reflection, his was a living reflection that wore a smirk and had cold, dark eyes.

"Hello, Joe. I thought I might show myself a little," the voice said. Panic drove Joe before his brain could restrain him. In one swift motion, his fist connected with the mirror, and there was a loud crack.

***

The sound of glass shattering drove Mr. Phillips from his sleep. Alarmed and alert, he scurried to his feet and tiptoed to his door. He felt his way around for the baseball bat beside the door, picked it up, and slipped out.

He walked lightly on his feet to avoid creaks that might alert the home intruder, searching the length and breadth of his house, listening for telltale sounds and sights, but there was nothing.

From the kitchen to the living room, Mr. Phillips checked every corner until he reached his son and daughter's adjoining rooms. First, he peered quietly into his daughter's room, but there was nothing out of the ordinary. Relieved, Mr. Phillips turned to his son's room. It was then he noticed the door was unlocked. A tinge of panic swept over him as he peeked into the open room.

There was no one in sight; no one there to answer when he called out his son's name.

Uneasy, Mr. Phillips glanced down the corridor of his three-bedroom apartment. Joe and Jeanne's rooms were separated from that of his and his wife's by the bathroom in the middle. That was when he realized he had omitted the bathroom in his security check.

He went to the bathroom where he met the door ajar. It was dark inside. Worried, Mr. Phillips pushed the door further open and stepped in. His left hand reflexively felt around the wall for the light switch. The light went on with a flick.

In the middle of the bathroom, his head hung in between his legs, was his son. A stir of emotion sent Mr. Phillips down onto his knees. "Joe... son, what's wrong?"

"It's nothing, Dad... it's nothing," Joe replied, hardly lifting his head.

Mr. Phillips inched closer to his son and wrapped his arms around him. He pulled his son into an embrace, with the latter breaking into a sob..

"I know you've been going through stuff. I know you've been trying to settle it on your own, son, but you don't have to. I'm here. Your mother and I are here for you," he said quietly, occasionally running his hands over Joe's hair.

HORRORS OF THE NIGHT

"I wish I could, Dad, but I can't." Joe whimpered. "I wish I could tell you both, but you won't understand. I can't explain it, but it keeps disturbing me... stalking me." He sniffed back some tears.

His son's words stung him, but Mr. Phillips shrugged the hurt off and listened. In moments like that, when Joe was overwhelmed, he knew that the best way to help was to listen quietly, and that was what he did.

***

"I... I keep hearing voices. I keep having these nightmares. I keep seeing things that are not real, things that never happened... or maybe they did, I don't even know. I don't know what's wrong with me," Joe protested.

"I know you wanted to ask, that you felt it would help me heal, but then you didn't bother. It's fine. I'll tell you.

HORRORS OF THE NIGHT

"I didn't change my SIM because I needed to forget my friends in school. There's no special package or plan for the SIM. I just needed it to... to escape," Joe said

"There's something—no, someone—stalking me," he said. He let out a huge sigh.

His dad stared silently, as if battling for the right words to say.

Joe forced a smile and kept speaking: "He claims to be me, claims to know all I know and feel everything I feel. He claims he's my... other half... an untethered soul or something, but he scares me, Dad.

"He's in my head, and he's in my phone. He makes me relive each nightmare every night, and that's why you find me awake at two a.m. every single day.

"I keep asking who he is and what he wants, but he keeps talking about being me and wanting me, and then some vague nonsense about things to do and achieve, as though he's trying to draw me into some cult," Joe added, and he sniffed to clear his nose.

HORRORS OF THE NIGHT

"That's all there is, Dad. That's all," he said, and he let out a heavy sigh.

His dad kept silent, watching him. After what felt like hours, his father chuckled. "Guess you're really a weak one, Joe," he said, his voice sounding eerily like the one Joe had been hearing. Shocked, Joe jerked away from his dad and stared. The image of his dad's face slowly shifted into the cold, dark face he'd seen in the mirror.

"You like my new look?" the voice queried, morphing its face back to that of his dad.

"Get away from me. Leave me alone… please!" Joe screamed, scurrying away from his "dad." His fingers stumbled on a big shard of glass, and they curled around it. He pointed the sharp end at his father, and in a dark, threatening tone, he repeated the words, "Leave me alone."

***

HORRORS OF THE NIGHT

Mr. Phillips was taken aback by his son's sudden jerk backward. Even worse was when he picked up a threatening shard of glass and pointed it at him. Afraid Joe might hurt himself, he tried shifting closer to his son, who not only glowered at him but tried slashing him with the glass shard. That was more than enough warning for him to maintain his distance.

The racket from the bathroom drew out his wife, she looked flustered from the disturbance.

"Honey, what's going on?" she queried. No sooner had she taken in the scene than her hands clasped to her mouth in shock. Tears welled up her eyes and fell down her cheeks. Not long after, she sank to her knees beside her husband, who held on to her lest she act on impulse. For all he knew, she might reach out to embrace her son, but in Joe's current state, that was too dangerous.

"Son, I know you're in a state right now, but you don't have to do anything. Look, we're only sitting here. We won't disturb you. We won't hurt you. Relax, son," Mr.

HORRORS OF THE NIGHT

Phillips said, raising his hands in surrender to calm to strained figure that was his son.

"Don't hurt yourself. Just relax, and let's stay here together. You'll get through this, and we'll help you through it all," he added.

His wife had slumped her head against his shoulders and was sobbing quietly as she stared at her son. Just like the episodes before, there was nothing much they could do other than wait out the mania and keep encouraging him with their words and presence.

~~~

Joe remained huddled in the corner, with the hand holding the glass shard stretched out before him. Although he felt tired and weak, he couldn't afford to sleep it off. A second tormentor had appeared, and this one had taken the face of his mother. He felt sickened by it. "I'm done with your games. I won't let you hurt me anymore," he'd said, spitting in their direction.

Neither of them moved, and he was grateful for that. He knew they would

HORRORS OF THE NIGHT

eventually carry out their usual torment. His life would flash before his eyes moments before he was swallowed up in pitch blackness to repeat the whole nightmare again. Though horrible, he wished they would get it over with. He needed to wake up. At least, he could feel a semblance of love and peace during the daytime when he wasn't asleep, and his tormentors no longer had a hold on him.

Joe's eyes blinked from the stress. His eyelids were heavy; they desperately wished for him to give in. He needed all the rest he could get, but then his fear was far more palpable than the need for sleep. In a moment of weakness, his eyes closed against his will. His tormentors moved as his vision blurred, and that was all.

***

Beep! Beep! Beep!

HORRORS OF THE NIGHT

Joe heard the sound, faint at first, then a little clearer. Stirring, he felt his eyes drift open to a world of white lights. He blinked to focus and realized he was staring into an array of fluorescent bulbs overhead. He brought his gaze down to see that he was on a white bed with leather straps on his arms. His hands were covered in bandages, and there was a thin tube attached to a vein in his left arm. Joe glanced around to find a lone figure, sleeping quietly in a seat beside his bed.

"Mom?" he called.

Her eyes flew open, and she drew her seat closer to him. "I'm here, dear. I'm here," she said. Her hand reached out to touch his forehead.

"Can I get a doctor in here? Phil," she called, then turned her gaze to her son.

"Mom, I'm sorry, " Joe blurted. His emotions raged, and he wasn't sure which one he felt more. "I'm sorry I couldn't be strong. I couldn't fight them off. I don't even know if I can fight anymore. I don't want to anymore." His tears fell freely as he spoke.

"Don't worry, honey, it's fine. I'm here. We'll get through this," she said, her voice quaking.

"We've been through this before. We can still push through. The doctors are saying something about meditating with local experts, that it'll be good for your mind and all that.

"You don't have to worry, son. You'll be fine. Your dad and I are with you through it all; just please, don't give up. Don't let go, swee—" It was as if she couldn't find the strength to go on. Joe knew he wasn't fine, and she was only trying to keep hope alive. He knew she could tell that he was afraid, there was no masking his emotions at that point. It was only a matter of time before he couldn't fight his demons anymore.

Chapter 5

"So what are you saying, Doctor? My son's crazy?" Mrs. Phillips asked. The thought of her son's condition forced her into another bout of tears and sniffling. Her husband, who was seated next to her, reflexively placed her hand in his and gave her a consoling squeeze.

"It's not every day we get patients like your son, Mr. and Mrs. Phillips. While the symptoms of dementia are clear, there are a few things that do not add up, Things we might need to take some time to monitor," said the doctor, slowly. He sounded as though he didn't want to aggravate the situation.

"Doctor," Mr. Phillips said.

"Joe staying a few more days or weeks in the hospital isn't a problem for us."

"But is there a chance Joe will be fine, no matter how little, Doctor?" queried Mr. Phillips.

His query left the doctor short of words, and both men were left staring at one another for way too long. Eventually, the doctor gave in and shut his eyes briefly. His action told more than the words he could muster. "As you know, Mr. Phillips, we're always committed to doing our best. We can take care of your son in the meantime—"

"Until there is nothing left to care for, right?" Mr. Phillips asked. His voice was hard.

Silence—punctuated by Mrs. Phillips' sobs—reigned in the doctor's office for what felt like hours.

"Thanks for your time, Doctor, but I don't think Joe will appreciate staying here. It might be best if we do the monitoring from home and give you a call should there be changes," Mr. Phillips said with a sigh. Joe had spent a week in the hospital with hardly any change, desperately begging that he be sent home. While the doctor was right about needing to keep an eye on Joe, the hospital just wasn't the right place for him.

"It's not a problem, Mr. Phillips. I understand how hard this must be for your family, and I'm willing to work with you on this," the doctor said, rising to his feet as he spoke.

"I'll have one of the nurses give you the prescription tabs for Joe. The suppressant tabs will keep Joe calm, while the pain meds will help curb his headaches. As for the insomnia, give him the sleep tabs in the prescribed dosage, and he won't have to worry about waking up for at least seven hours," the doctor explained.

Mr. Phillips nodded and stretched out his hand, to which the doctor extended his own.

Mrs. Phillips rose quietly beside her husband and wiped her tears with a hanky she pulled from her handbag.

The couple stepped carefully out of the office with the doctor, who led them to one of his standby nurses, gave a few instructions, and sent them off to the pharmacy.

***

Joe's eyes lit up at the news of leaving the hospital. He was the one to break the news. From changing out of his hospital gown into his own clothes and finally getting into the car for the drive back home, Joe felt a sense of relief wash over him. Being at the hospital hadn't been the best option for him. Rather, it had left him vulnerable. The voice had kept taunting him with its sinister laughter, reinforcing his nightmares.

Although he wasn't utterly safe from the voice at home, he knew he was better off there. At the very least, he would find strength and hope there, compared to the hospital that seemed confining, with its white walls, sterile smell, and routine nurses whose smiles were no less reassuring. He never saw them for their smiles; he saw his tormentors instead.

HORRORS OF THE NIGHT

The drive back home was quiet and uneventful, and he was glad for the silence. Once they'd made it up the driveway, he sighed, looked over at his parents, and said, "Thank you." No further words were exchanged as they got out of the car and made their way indoors. As far as he was concerned, his bed was calling him.

***

"Well, well, look who decided to wake up," Joe's dad said jokingly. The rest of the family was seated in the living room with the TV on when Joe stepped groggily from his room. It was a few minutes before eight pm, and that meant Joe had missed dinner. For what it was worth, he was relieved to see his son so relaxed.

"There's nothing like a good sleep, I can tell," he added, to which Joe smiled. It had seemed genuine, with no trace of weakness or fear.

HORRORS OF THE NIGHT

"Come here, Joe. Come sit with me," his wife beckoned to their son.

Mr. Phillips protested, saying, "Don't be selfish, hon—"

"Come sit with us," his mom said, turning to Joe. The little drama kept Joe's smile intact as he scuttled over to the couch and sat on the rug between his parents.

The three of them sat in silence as they flipped through the channels and settled on a show. After an hour-plus of TV, Mrs. Phillips' eyes closed, and she was soon fast asleep, her head leaning on her husband's shoulders. Joe was left with his father in the night's silence.

"How are you feeling?" his dad asked quietly.

"I feel better. Guess all I needed was a proper sleep," he said. He chuckled at the end.

"That's good, Joe, that's good," his dad replied.

HORRORS OF THE NIGHT

Joe took a moment to turn to his dad. His dad had a smile on his face.

***

Daylight came, and Joe found himself sprawled on his bed. The night had been without the usual nightmares, and for that, he was relieved. He did, however, feel odd in the far edge of his gut, as though he anticipated something sinister.

Since he'd left the hospital about two weeks before, he hadn't had to deal with his nightmares. His cellphone was well within reach, but he hardly touched it. He was mostly uninterested in his phone than afraid. His parents, who'd suggested keeping it from him, seemed to relax when they noticed he had barely touched the phone since he'd returned. Anytime they'd spoken to him about it, he usually shrugged and said he just wasn't into his phone anymore.

"Besides, it's not like I have a thousand people calling me or who I have to call," he often added to justify his break from his phone. So far, he only had one person he could call, and he'd resorted to using either of his parents' cellphones when he felt like it. Kyle, having received calls from two different numbers, had grown used to his friend's new means of reaching out.

Now that he thought of it, his gaze fell to his phone and lingered there a little more than he'd wished.

"Not today," he muttered, shrugging his lingering gaze.

He took off to the bathroom and made quick work of brushing his teeth, followed by his routine face washing. With the tap running, he scooped water to his face and pressed his hands to his eyes; the water was soothing.

Joe exhaled and brought a few more handfuls of water to his face, and let it trickle slowly down his cheeks. He opened his eyes. His reflection in the bathroom mirror caught his attention—it was wearing a smirk, but Joe wasn't.

Joe blinked. The smirk on the reflection relaxed, and it displayed the same curious gaze as Joe. He blinked again and followed it with a wave of his hand to ease his fear. He could have sworn his reflection had taken on an expression of its own. Joe shut his eyes and let his mind relax.

Upon returning to his room, Joe's eyes drifted to the top of his bedside table where his phone laid idle. He turned to leave his room but no sooner had he taken a step out than he flipped back into his room.

He muttered about the experience as he snatched the phone from his bedside table—it had turned on. A few seconds later, and his phone was fully booted. In no time, he was on his dialer, tapping out a phone number. "Here we go. " He sighed and made the call.

Silence.

After a few more tries, Joe finally gave up. Deep down, he felt a stir of hope. Maybe he was finally free of his demons.

HORRORS OF THE NIGHT

86

TOM COLEMAN

Chapter 6

"Well, well, you're looking good, Joe," he said to himself as he examined his reflection in the bathroom mirror. The tap was running endlessly in the sink, and the light bulb hanging above his head flickered at his every word. It was a little past midnight.

"Nothing like a good wash to clear the head," he said, splashing a handful of water on his face.

"So, what's it going to be tonight? Hm—maybe a little TV?" The water trickled down his face in tiny drops. Without a second thought to wipe his face, Joe turned for the bathroom door.

Upon getting to the living room, he crashed on the couch and picked up the TV's remote. A few clicks afterward, he settled on an off-air station. "Ahh, yes—midnight classic it is," he said with a little clap.

HORRORS OF THE NIGHT

"What are you doing?" a low, sleepy voice queried.

Joe's eyes darted in the direction of the voice.

Jeanne was staring at him, a puzzled expression on her face. It was as though she couldn't decide whether to yield to the lure of sleep or query the sight before her.

"Ah, Jeanne—Guess you finally decided to come join me. I was waiting," Joe said happily. He beckoned her with a hand gesture and said, "Come on—come, join your big brother."

Jeanne yawned in response, made her way groggily to the couch, and huddled close to Joe. She rested her head on his shoulder and wrapped her arm around his. "What are we watching?" she asked.

Joe looked at her sweetly and said, "Take a guess."

Jeanne rubbed her eyes and looked at the TV screen. A frown slowly crept onto her face. As though frightened by what she saw, she turned to Joe. "I don't like this movie," she said, her voice conveying fear.

"Really?" Joe asked brightly. "But I watch it every night." He added, "Come on—it's not that bad, Jeannie."

"But he's scared. They'll do bad things to him," Jeanne said apprehensively.

"Hmm, maybe you're right. Maybe they'll do bad things to him, but it's pretty fun," Joe replied. "Oh, here's my favorite part: the chants." Joe turned his gaze back to the static on the TV screen.

As though responding to Joe's expectations, the TV screen flickered. The white noise of the static changed to a more discernible sound. The chant of "Teatime," repeated through the TV's speakers, growing louder with each passing second.

Joe looked on with glee while his younger sister cowered where she sat, squeezing closer to him.

"Make it stop," Jeanne pleaded, tugging at Joe's arm.

HORRORS OF THE NIGHT

He turned to look at her wearing a wide, unnatural grin. "Is Jeannie scared?" he whispered.

She nodded, her face buried into his arm.

"Don't worry, Jeannie—your big brother's here. It'll be over soon," he said, planted a kiss on her head.

***

"Good morning, Mom—what's for breakfast?" Joe asked once he'd stepped into the kitchen.

His mom was washing dirty dishes.

Jeanne was standing at the counter next to her, but the moment she saw him, she scurried into the corner.

"Jeanne, no running in the kitchen," Mrs. Phillips said, turning to her youngest child, who was trying to make herself scarce.

"Sorry," Jeanne said from her hiding spot. "Joe is scary," she added.

HORRORS OF THE NIGHT

Joe and his mom exchanged perplexed glances at her words. Joe felt even more confused. "But I didn't do anything," he said, raising his hands.

His mom stopped tending to the dishes, went over to Jeanne, and said sweetly, "Come on, Jeannie—you love your big brother, don't you?"

"Yes," she replied quietly, "but he's scaring me."

"How?" Joe said aloud.

His mom held up a finger. "Talk to me, sweetie. What did Joe do?"

"He was watching a scary show on TV. They were doing bad things to him on TV," she said, playing with her fingers as she spoke.

"The show was really scary, huh?" their mom queried.

Jeanne nodded.

"So, it's the show that's scary, and not Joe, right?" she asked again.

Jeanne nodded her head, but she glanced quickly at Joe and shook her head. "Joe is scary. He was looking at me in a bad way," she mumbled.

"Oh, really?" their mom said. "When did he look at you in a bad way?"

"Last night, " she said quietly.

Mrs. Phillips stared at her daughter for a while and then sighed. "Don't worry about it, okay, Jeannie?" she offered. "He was just playing, and I'll ground him for that, okay?" she said. Her voice rose a little at the latter part of the sentence so he would know she meant business, and it wasn't an empty threat.

Jeanne nodded and reluctantly allowed her mom to pull her away from her hiding spot. She avoided looking directly at Joe until he'd left the kitchen with a bottle of water.

***

HORRORS OF THE NIGHT

Mrs. Phillips knew that Joe had no idea about what his younger sister was talking about in the kitchen. He'd played it according to his usual script of saying nothing and waiting for her to resolve whatever misunderstanding what going on between him and his younger sister. This mostly happened after she'd succeeded in coaxing Jeanne to speak about whatever was wrong, but on that day, Jeanne had hardly budged. Apart from what she'd said in the kitchen, she wasn't forthcoming with the full story of what Joe had done.

Nightfall came, and there was still nothing from Jeanne concerning what she'd said about Joe. For most of the day, Jeanne had avoided him totally. She'd even gone as far as staying cooped up in her room.

"Relax, hon—she'll be fine, " her husband had said when it was time to go to sleep, but she couldn't shake the fear she'd seen in her daughter's eyes. It wasn't like the other times Joe had pranked her. It was much darker. As though there was, indeed, something in Joe that scared her.

HORRORS OF THE NIGHT

***

A lone chime sounded in Joe's room. Joe's cellphone screen lit up. The time read 00:00.

Another chime and Joe's screen flickered. A message popped up in the notifications tray that read, "Wake up, Joe. "

Joe's body sat up in the bed as if on instinct. His eyes stirred, and he opened them slowly. They were dark and foreboding. He craned his neck slowly toward his phone. His hand followed his gaze, and it hovered slightly above the phone. The lone light from the phone's screen cast an eerie glow on his open palm.

He picked up the phone and clicked on the new message. The sender was none other than his phone number. A smile crept over his face.

Joe rose to his feet and left his room. Though he had no destination in mind, he wound up in the kitchen and sat on a tall stool by the kitchen counter. Joe looked around, but he settled on staring directly ahead. His fingers tapped on the countertop in unison to the sound of the wall clock on the kitchen wall.

He stayed that way for ten full minutes, staring ahead and tapping away before breaking out of his reverie. His gaze drifted to the knife block. His body followed his gaze, and within seconds, he was standing before the rack, his eyes roaming from knife to knife.

"Clean and simple, that's all you need," he muttered. His fingers wrapped around a carving knife, and he pulled it slowly from the block. There was a flash before his eyes, a picture of the knife being pulled from the block covered in fresh bloodstains.

Joe smiled at the thought.

He raised the knife to his face and trailed a finger across the knife's edge, feeling its sharpness.

Joe nodded, took a few steps back, turned, and walked out of the kitchen. He made his way to the foyer, between to house's three rooms. He moved towards his parents room, and stopped at their door. There, he let out a sigh.

He placed his left hand on the doorknob, turned, and heard, "Joe?" coming from behind him.

Joe tucked the knife into the shorts he'd worn to sleep, draped his shirt over it carefully, and straightened his posture. Then, he turned to his little sister and smiled. "How are you, princess?" he asked.

Jeanne took a step back and muttered, "Fine."

Joe noticed her retreat and said, "Shh. Don't worry, Jeannie. I'm your big brother. I'm not going to hurt you."

"But... but you're scary," Jeanne said.

"That's why you didn't play with me yesterday, huh? You couldn't even look at me?" Joe asked.

Jeanne nodded.

HORRORS OF THE NIGHT

"It's okay. I'm sorry I scared you. I didn't mean to," Joe said, taking a step closer.

Jeanne looked hesitant, but she waited till he came within her reach.

Joe crouched low to her eye level, shut his eyes for a moment, and then opened them again. "See? It's still me, your big brother," he said, looking at her.

Jeanne stared at him with a worried look on her face. She sighed and said, "Yeah, I guess it's you."

"Of course, it's me, Jeannie. And I'm here if you need me," he offered. "So, do you want to talk about it?" he asked after a few moments had passed in silence.

Jeanne nodded.

At this, he sat down on the floor and leaned against the wall. He indicated that Jeanne should do the same, and he put an arm around her after she'd complied.

"I know you weren't lying. About me walking," Jeanne started.

HORRORS OF THE NIGHT

Joe's mind traveled to the time he'd returned from school: the sleepwalking episode.

"I was dreaming, and then I saw you bring me in and tuck me in, but—"

"But what?" Joe asked.

"You... you came back and stood in my room. You were looking at me like the other night," she said.

Joe kept quiet and allowed her to continue speaking.

"Then, you left, and you left my door open. I was afraid, so I didn't want to get out of bed," she explained.

Joe recalled her denial about sleepwalking, but the part about him returning to her room escaped him. He had no memory of doing such a thing. Neither was he aware of a second night on which he'd stared at her. "But you said you didn't, " Joe said uncertainly.

Jeanne said, "No, I thought I was dreaming."

HORRORS OF THE NIGHT

"Oh," Joe said thoughtfully. "It happens like that all the time, huh? You dream about walking, and then you actually do?"

Jeanne nodded. "But then I forget," she added after a while.

"Huh?"

"When I wake up, I don't remember dreaming or walking," she explained.

Joe nodded. He understood what she was talking about.

While Jeanne kept talking about her sleepwalking episodes, he felt an unsettling stir in the pit of his stomach. His hands twitched at intervals, and for a moment, he swore the knife hidden in his shorts was getting hot enough to burn his skin.

"That's why I was afraid of you yesterday. Because I know I wasn't dreaming, and it wasn't you," Jeanne said.

Joe, who'd been focused on restraining the unsettling feeling in his gut, snapped back to reality. "What did you say?" he queried.

HORRORS OF THE NIGHT

"The other night. I had a bad dream, and then I woke up," Jeanne said.

Joe made a hand gesture, encouraging her to keep talking.

"I went to the bathroom, then I heard the TV, so I came out to check. I thought that maybe, I'd see dad or mom, but I saw you, instead," Jeanne explained. "But... but then, it wasn't you. It looked like you, but it wasn't you. It was a bad person. A very bad and scary you," Jeanne said.

Joe's breath caught in his throat as Jeanne explained what had transpired the night before. He had no memory of what had happened, but as she spoke, images began forming in his head: his reflection in the mirror; the trickling of water off his face; the static from the TV; the chant.

Jeanne had been there, but that wasn't what had sent him jumping up to his feet and racing to his room. Visions of him waking up at midnight poured in. Realization dawned on him in flashes. He had been sleeping too well for weeks, and that was why he felt uneasy. The silence hadn't been what he'd hoped. It hadn't been because he was finally free of the voice, the one who'd claimed to be his other-self.

Joe gasped for air as his mind pieced the influx of thoughts together. He had been waking up at midnight since he'd returned from the hospital, but it hadn't been him who was conscious during those moments at midnight. It had been his other-self. The untethered being that had been speaking in his head and through his phone number.

Joe stumbled from the floor to his feet and on to his room. He pulled out the red hot knife and threw it as far as he could. His hand reached for his cellphone, and he dialed quickly.

Call not connected.

"Come on," Joe exclaimed as he tried redialing his phone number to no avail. Three more unconnected redials, and his phone flung from his hand. But the crash of the phone into the far wall hardly registered in his mind when he noticed Jeanne standing in his doorway, open-mouthed and confused.

"Wh... what's wrong?" she asked.

Unsure of how to answer, Joe shook his head. "Something's really wrong Jeanne," he started, "but I'm going to find out what, and I'm going to fix it." He sighed, and took a few careful steps toward her, took her hand, and led her out of his room.

***

While Joe did his best to distract himself from the eerie feeling in his gut, his mind kept replaying Jeanne's words and the images of each night he'd been awake but not in control of his consciousness. That night would likely have followed the same pattern with a lethal result if Jeanne had not woken when she did. For all he knew, the knife hadn't been for fun, and he definitely hadn't planned on entering his parents' room for a midnight chat. He hadn't thought much about it, but now that he did, his other side hadn't been joking about getting what and who he wanted. He'd sounded dark and threatening, and now Joe understood those words for what they'd meant. Joe was dealing with a malevolent entity who could turn him into a monster and ruin his home, but he had no idea why.

Joe sat beside Jeanne's bed, waiting for her to fall asleep as she eyed him through concerned, sleepy eyes. At different times, he noticed her staring at him, but in the end, sleep won out.

Although Joe had no idea about how to handle the situation, he felt a nagging feeling that he needed to contact his darker self and maybe strike a deal. Giving the numbness he'd felt in his mind since he'd gone on the meds, the calls no longer connecting, and his phone totally smashed, he was at a loss.

"The mirror," he realized. While he had discarded the last experience with the mirror as his mind playing tricks on him, he understood it was his only option, so Joe made his way to the bathroom, turned on the tap, and carried out his routine wash.

***

"Well, well, look who's decided to call me," the sinister voice said with a chuckle.

Joe stared at his reflection in the mirror. The only difference was in their eyes—Joe looked weary and fearful, while his untethered self had a threatening aura.

Joe swallowed. "Why are you doing this?" he asked quietly.

"Is there ever a reason for what we do?" the voice replied.

Joe gritted his teeth at the evasive response.

"But I'll humor you," it added. "Free will is either taken, or it is given. There is more to you than you realize, but you have failed to yield. It is only wise that I take what is mine—"

HORRORS OF THE NIGHT

"I don't belong to you," Joe muttered.

His reflection arched an eyebrow.

Joe said even louder, "You don't own me!"

His other self looked perplexed for a split second before it burst out laughing.

Enraged, Joe threw a fist at the mirror. Its impact caused a sizeable crack on the mirror's surface.

His other self wore a clear expression of shock at the sudden move. "Joe," it started. The mirror cracked further. With each word it tried to say, the mirror cracked further until the pieces shattered and crumbled into the sink.

Exhausted, Joe crumpled to his knees on the bathroom floor.

Hurried footsteps approached the bathroom, and for a moment before his eyes closed, he saw his mom and dad rush in.

***

HORRORS OF THE NIGHT

Ever since his previous encounter in the bathroom, Joe had burned his SIM card and thrown his phone thrown in the trashcan. With his phone, SIM, and bathroom mirror gone, and his meds ensuring he no longer woke up during the night, Joe felt peace. When he was ready, he told his parents what he'd been battling with. Although the looks on their faces said they'd found it his story hard to believe, they agreed not to replace the bathroom's mirror.

Days turned into weeks and weeks into months with no unsettling feelings in the pit of his stomach. Although Joe had told his parents that all was well, they had gone the extra mile to bring a priest into the house. After a few uncomfortable conversations, the priest blessed the entire house by sprinkling Holy Water. Joe was offered communion bread and wine and given a few scripture verses to say aloud before going to sleep. Joe obliged his parents and the priest and soon found that he could sleep without the meds on which he'd heavily relied. The scriptures

HORRORS OF THE NIGHT

were working, and he relayed that message to the priest, who congratulated him on being free of the demons that had troubled him.

"But remember, Joe—demons are jealous beings who stop at nothing to regain what they have lost. Be careful not to let your mind wander. Avoid thinking of your past or the voice you once heard, lest you call to him and be taken back into bondage," the priest had instructed Joe. True to the man's words, when Joe found his mind wandering, he began to feel uneasy. And that reminded him to restrain his thoughts and let go of the past.

***

Joe remained safely at home, gradually forgetting about the horrors of the past, but his untethered self remained very much present. Though separate from Joe due to measures put in place by the priest and the young man himself, the other side of Joe watched and waited, growing more vengeful as the months passed.

HORRORS OF THE NIGHT

Time passed rather swiftly, and Joe was on to the next phase of his life: college. He reconnected with Kyle via a new SIM he'd taken to the priest to bless. Together, he and Kyle applied to a list of colleges and kept their fingers crossed for updates. Their admissions in sync, the young men looked forward to a bout of joy. There was, however, someone else biding his time, counting on their joy.

***

Drip…drip…drip.

Water trickled down Joe's face. His eyes were closed, his breathing even.

"We meet again, Joe," an uncanny voice said.

Joe's eyes darted opened to meet those of his reflection in the mirror. His other self stared at him, dead in the eyes. Unlike the last time, its eyes were pitch black. Dark veins extended from his eyes across his face.

HORRORS OF THE NIGHT

"You've been a very stubborn one, Joe," it said.

Joe reacted quickly, and he launched a fist into the mirror. Before his fist connected, he felt an unimaginable force restrain it, inches away from the mirror.

"No, no, you don't get to do that again," his darker self retorted.

Joe pulled his hands from the force of the mirror and turned to escape. He took a step toward the bathroom door and felt a force lift him off the ground.

"You should have listened," he heard his untethered self say. In one swift motion, he was slammed into the ground, and his head crashed through the ceramic sink.

There was silence.

Drip…drip…drip.

Joe felt the familiar sensation of water, only it wasn't the water it had been in his dreams; it was his blood.

HORRORS OF THE NIGHT

***

The news of the boy that had been found dead in the college bathroom traveled fast. Joe Phillips's body was found in a flooded bathroom with a sizeable crater beneath it. The autopsy report attributed the cause of death to a domestic accident. The medical examiner had theorized that Joe had fallen and broken not just his head but the bathroom sink.

What neither the police nor the autopsy experts could not understand was what had formed the crater beneath him. It looked as if Joe Phillips had been thrown high and smashed into the floor by an inexplicable force, only they could not determine what might have had enough force to do that.

"He was my friend. My best friend, " Kyle reported when giving an interview on behalf of the grieving family. "We went to school, studied, and graduated together. The things we went through together… and now he's gone, just like that." Kyle's voice broke. His tears flowed freely.

"There's something dark out there, something the cops aren't telling. I know it because Joe kept trying to run from it. He told me about it. First, it was in his dreams, and then the calls, and then the hallucinations. " He figured he'd said enough. Though others might guess that his grief had silenced him, the truth was that Kyle's tongue had frozen against his will. It hadn't been grief, but something else, something that didn't want him to say all he knew. It was the same thing he'd once told Joe had been nothing more than his thoughts gone wild.

Kyle kept quiet. He was there to grieve with Joe's family, and that was what he did.

When it was time to return to his parents, Mr. Phillips offered to drive him home. "It's the least I can do," Mr. Phillips had said.

Kyle accepted the offer, and the duo drove in silence until Kyle was home. As Mr. Phillips drove out of sight, Kyle felt a buzz in his trouser pockets. He pulled out his phone and blinked twice; it was his own phone number calling him.

THE CURSE OF HERNANDEZ
PART THREE

TOM COLEMAN

HORRORS NEXT DOOR

114

TOM COLEMAN

CHAPTER FIVE: Pain

For Christina, the first wave came in the form of pins and needles. She looked at her skin and saw needles all over, but she managed to hold her scream. It didn't hurt that much, and she was grateful for that. The problem started when it legit began to hurt.

"Carlos, you said it was just in our m—" but Carlos was no place to be found. Had the house been able to separate them so quickly? It was as if the house sucked on their fears and guilt even faster than before. It was unreal.

"How are they doing this? What is happening?" Christina's brain could no longer function optimally by then due to the excruciating pain. She knew she had to overcome this by herself. Hiding behind Carlos would get her nowhere. It was a sickening scenario unlike any other, and Carlos had his own demons to fight, some of which she did not even know about. She had to get out of this mental hell on her own.

"They're just needles...they're just needles. Keep it together," Christina repeated to herself. With each needle prick she felt, Christina reminded herself that her pain was in her mind.

"Look at what you did to me," Susan said, standing with her head in her hand. Christina could not believe the sight before her. It was too much.

"That wasn't what happened." She was letting her emotions get in the way again, luring her deeper into the mindfuck. "My God."

"God isn't yours, and he isn't going to save you."

"So? Would it have made a difference?" Susan inquired.

Her decapitated head rested on her hands as it spoke in the most disturbing of ways. It wasn't real… none of it was real. Christina knew it, but it was still a scary and unnerving sight to behold. How could that thing do this to the poor girl's memory?

"Why are you doing this? Susan does not deserve this." Christina was confused. Was it the house or the ghosts instead? She and Carlos needed to get to the suitcase as quickly as possible before they were consumed by the creatures' nefarious attacks.

The entity masquerading as Susan walked closer to Christina, but she backed up. Christina could practically feel the terror on her face.

As the ghost came closer, it grew more disfigured but maintained Susan's general shape.

"Once, there was a woman. A beautiful, strong woman." The headless body kept growing, as did the head. "She bought a house thinking it was a bargain. Little did she know he would come to watch her sleep. Who, you say? The pitch-black man who came again and again. It got so bad, Heather could only weep." By then, the ghoul was right in front of a petrified Christina. The head continued to grow in size as the mouth spoke. Christina was hanging onto her sanity for dear life, but it wasn't working at the moment. Her fear covered any coherence her mind might have like a blanket.

The pitch-black man? That big, huge monster that could not get into the room but lurked right outside? Who was he, and what was this story she was being told? Christina could barely take in all the information she was being told. Who could and be expected to retain it when they were that scared and in pain? The needles were still incredibly painful, but there was something even more unnerving and creepy about the headless demon holding the head of the girl she'd killed that made the needle pain subside a little.

The fiendish creature raised the head of what still looked partly like Susan up to Christina's face, positioning it to face her.

"Do you know what happened to Heather?" the head inquired.

Christina just stared fearfully. There was nothing more she could do than look at it and try to calm down. She had to get her mind under control, but it wasn't working.

"As things got harder, she retreated deeper into the room. He couldn't get in, and that was enough for her to remain inside."

"What… what kind of… what are you saying?" Christina said to the head. The fact she was being talked to and responding to a giant head was ridiculous, but it was her reality. Wait… no. Christina cautioned herself—it was not real. There was no reality. Everything was a simulation in her mind, a metaphysical creation emanating from the house's ability to see her memories and weaknesses.

"I wonder where Heather is right now?" the head said, looking to the corner as if trying to remember.

"Please, just let us go," Christina pleaded.

The head laughed after hearing that. "Heather used to say that. It didn't do anything, though, and it won't do anything for you, either."

The needles continued boring into her skin, leading Christina to scream in agony. She yelled as loud as she could, reacting to the immeasurable hurt coming from her pain. "Why… why are you doing this? What is this house?"

"You will know soon enough about our tragic fate."

She could only hear the voice of the fiend. The pain had caused her to fall to the ground and face the floor, so she couldn't see it. Was this the end, the way her life and dreams would come crashing down? Christina thought about a lot of things at that moment. Could she have reconciled or made the relationship better with her parents?

Would she ever know the experience and joy of motherhood? More importantly, Christina would lose the chance to share her love with the man of her dreams.

"No," the determined woman yelled, enduring the pain and getting to her feet. "I will not let you win. I won't let this sick house prevail. You won't have me, and you won't have my husband, either." She looked up, but the apparition was no longer before her.

The needles still pricked her skin. Even breathing was painful, and every step she took felt like a wild animal bite. She knew it was not real, and all she needed to do was to stand her ground and be steadfast. To Christina's surprise, the more she held onto the belief that everything happening was not real, the less painful the needle pricks.

"I will get through this and reach my husband. You are in my way. Get out!" There was such gumption in her words that it actually helped to clear the darkness a bit, and Christina spotted a figure ahead of her. It could be a lot of things, but she chose the best option.

"Carlos," she called, and she noticed the pain from the needles was gone. She smiled and scoffed, relieved her mind had been strong enough to fight back and win.

When she looked back up, a needle inserted itself into her eye. "AARRRRRRRRRGGHH!" she cried.

Carlos didn't know where Christina had gone, but the worst possible thing that could happen right then—especially for Christina—was for them to be separated. She was mentally fragile, and he needed to be there for her. The familiar sound of the guitar reverberated through the dark space, and Carlos finally remembered where it was from.

"So, that's what it is, huh?" he said, facing his sister. Carlos, however, knew the thing on the chair facing him and holding the guitar was not his sister.

"Yes."

"That sound was the note Rosa kept playing when she learned how to play the guitar," Carlos said, and the demon nodded. Just remembering how she had failed at her early lessons made Carlos smile. He never liked to remember much about his sister due to how painful it was, but this memory brought a smile to his face. Rosa had played the same old note, bothering him. Oh, what he'd give to go back to those glorious days. Sure, there were many other problems—like the crime and the lack of basic amenities—but it didn't matter because he'd had her, and she'd had him.

"You think this will do… what? Make me break down and cry? I already know this is not real, so why don't you just let me go?"

HORRORS NEXT DOOR

The entity laughed out loud, its mouth widening abnormally. Carlos stared at her in confusion. He was surprised at not being tortured, but he knew he had to be on guard. Anything could happen in that blasted house.

"You honestly believe you can escape?" The voice had changed, becoming less like his sister's and more sinister. "Why do you feel so guilty about Rosa?"

"Stop it." Carlos felt himself grow agitated, which was the last thing he wanted.

The ghost smiled, finally having found an entry into his strongly fortified mind. "Let's see, shall we?"

Carlos was suddenly standing in his childhood home. It was bad. It was really bad. The sounds of multiple gunshots went off outside, and he knew what that meant. In the room, Carlos saw him and his sister hugging each other under the bed.

"Mom wasn't around, was she?" the ghost said from behind him.

He turned to see a hellish-looking ghoul floating in the air.

Carlos dropped to the ground in fear.

The ghoul completely ignored him and focused on Carlos's past. "Of course, she wasn't around," it said. "She had to work twice as hard to put food on the table for the two of you."

"Stop this," Carlos warned sternly, but he was surely in no position to warn anyone or anything.

"And we can't forget the humiliating beatings you received from your drunken father." The setting changed to another from Carlos's childhood, one he remembered all too well. He had come back at night to find his father beating his mother. Rosa could only beg him to stop from a distance—who knew what he might do to her if she intervened?

"Rosa couldn't do anything," Carlos said, transfixed to the scenery before him, lulled deeper into the clutches of the nefarious house. Past guilt and trauma were always better forms of pain to manipulate an individual than present and physical ones.

"Yes… yes," the ghoul spurred him on as he watched his mother being kicked. "You had to intervene, didn't you?"

"Yes. I ran and pushed him off her with all my strength." As he said it, the scene unfolded in front of him.

Carlos's dad frowned at the young boy with so much anger, it brought Carlos back to that moment in his head, and he relived the fear that had coursed through him back then.

"And your father beat you until you were near death for that, didn't he?"

Carlos watched his mother and sister cry as they watched him getting beaten…

until his sister crashed a large vase on their father's head.

"He wasn't going to stop," Carlos said, trying to explain why it had not been her fault. "I was almost unconscious. I might have died. She had always been a great sister, and she looked out for me. There was no way Rosa was going to let me die."

"Then why did you let her die?"

The question hit him hard. He did not want to have that conversation. Carlos rarely talked about it.

The setting changed to another time in his life, when he had come back from what looked like a brawl, his knuckles partially bloodied.

"As you grew older, you wanted to help your mother out, is that it?" It kept speaking into his ear.

Carlos was breaking down mentally. It was not what he'd wanted. He hadn't wanted to bring his mother any pain or sorrow. He'd just been a young kid, trying to be the man of the house after they'd killed for him and saved his life.

"They reported it to the police as self-defense, which it was," Carlos responded without blinking, fully immersed in the illusion before him because it felt like reality. The adult man watched his younger self treat his mother and sister badly. Carlos knew why he'd done it—he'd wanted to prove himself so badly it took him to dark places, and when his mom had talked to him about it, he'd dismissed her harshly and said it was all for them to survive.

"You beat people up, stole, lied, and did all other horrible things while telling yourself it was for them."

"Stop." A tear escaped his eye as he was forced to watch all of the terrible things he had done. Carlos had forgotten about the fact they were in a haunted house or that his wife was probably suffering at that very moment. They had found his fulcrum, his weak point. Now that it had been hit, the young man was falling apart.

"I'm sorry, Mom," he said, trying to console his crying mother while the younger version of himself simply walked past her.

"We should strive to be better, Carlos," Rosa had said to him, but Carlos didn't want to hear it. He hadn't noticed that he had been so drawn into the powers of the house that he had entered the body of his younger self.

"Leave me alone. It will all make sense when we make it out of here and get a better life," he responded to her. "Everything I am doing—"

"Is for us, right?" Rosa finished, looking like she was tired of that same old excuse. "This life you are living… it will catch up to you one day, Carlos," she said, walking away. "I just hope you are able to see the end of the tunnel you are striving so hard for us to reach. I hope we see it, too."

He was in tears. It had been so painful. He didn't like to confront the role his lifestyle and stubbornness had played in her demise.

"I'm... sorry." Carlos fell to the ground, crying, barely registering that he was inhabiting his younger body. "It's all my fault."

"You killed me," the image of Rosa said.

Carlos was so utterly transfixed, he thought it was really her. "It wasn't the rival gang to the one you joined; it was you. When you joined those guys and got into all that crap, you invited attacks on you, and by extension, on us."

He couldn't even counter what had been said because he'd believed it. Somewhere deep within him, he'd always housed blame for not heeding her warnings.

He kept on going and moving forward but leaving his family behind.

"But by the time you came back for them," the ghoul whispered into his ear. For Carlos, it was as if he was hearing his innermost thoughts, "one of them was gone."

The room changed to the day he came home to find her lifeless body on the floor. "No, no, no, no—I don't want to see this! I don't wanna fucking see this!" Carlos closed his eyes, but it was as if his lids were transparent. Even with his eyes closed, he could see it. "Argh! Stop!" He was in the body of his younger self, watching like a passenger as he came home and yelled for his sister. He had heard they'd found out where he'd lived and attacked his home as payback for a series of problems the group he was in had caused them.

"There she is," the ghost said, as if satisfied. The entity stood beside Rosa's lifeless body as Carlos held her in his arms. There were bullet wounds all over her body.

She'd been barraged by gunshots, probably from a drive-by.

"Mom wasn't around, was she?" the voice reverberated in his ear. "She was out trying to keep food on the table. Meanwhile, in your attempt to protect your family by joining the gang, you guaranteed its end. It… was… all… you."

"I'm… I'm so sorry. I didn't mean for this to happen. Please, come back!"

"You should pay for this. You have a happy life right now while she is in the dirt. You don't deserve happiness. She did, but you took that from her."

The darkness crept further into his psyche, and Carlos blamed himself. He should be dead. It should have been him. He was broken.

"Don't you want to see her and apologize for what you did to her?"

"Yes, I do. I really do."

"Then take this and come and meet me," Rosa said, smiling. She handed a knife to Carlos.

He gazed at the knife for a minute as if in a daze. "Okay."

CHAPTER FOUR: I can't believe this

Christina yelled and screamed louder than she had ever screamed before. It was so painful having the needle in her eye that she fell to the floor, screaming as blood gushed out of it profusely.

"I thought this was not real," she screamed to herself.

The ghosts laughed. Christina thought she could hear nearly a thousand laughs.

She looked up, and with her working eye, saw several ghosts walking toward her. There were that many ghosts? All of them lived in the house? What exactly was this gnarly, scary dungeon masquerading as a house? "What is going on here? Why are there so many of you?"

"Join us and find out," one of the ghosts said, looking fierce. They hovered above the ground as they surrounded her.

Christina took a deep breath and thought. She had to open her mind to the fact that what she was experiencing was not real. The needle in her eye did not exist. Despite the excruciating pain, it was not real. None of it was. Sure, the ghosts had to be real, but the mindfuck was all in her head, and if it was directed by her own beliefs, that meant she could also control the outcome. She had the power, not them. Maybe she was wrong, but Christina did not care. She was going to get out of there and find her husband or die trying.

HORRORS NEXT DOOR

She took a deep breath and shut her eyes, even the one with the needle in it. When she opened them back up, one word came out of her mouth: "Leave."

In an instant, the atmospheric doom and gloom, the darkness, and the ghosts disappeared, and she realized that she was still in the bedroom, as was Carlos.

Wait… Carlos? He was holding a knife and was about to stab himself.

"Carlos," Christina yelled, running over to him to stop him from stabbing himself. He was pretty strong, though, so the task proved difficult to accomplish. She kept yelling his name in an attempt to try to get him to stop his suicide attempt.

***

"What?" Carlos finally muttered, hearing a faint but familiar voice call his name from a distance. His hand gripped the knife tightly, but something was stopping him.

"You have to do it now, brother," Rosa said to him hastily.

"But that voice—"

"Do it," she yelled, looking a bit sinister as her corneas were turning red. "Suffer as we did! Become us! Become trapped!"

"This… isn't real, is it?" Carlos said, finally coming back to himself, morphing back into his adult body. He looked at himself, got some bearing on where he was, and dropped the knife.

"Carlos!"

The voice was louder this time, and he immediately pinpointed it as Christina's. He got up and looked around, trying to find her.

HORRORS NEXT DOOR

"You need to end it now," Rosa pressed. "We can be together, Carlos."

Carlos Hernandez closed his eyes and envisioned the great, kind, happy sister he knew. She would never have wanted him dead before he'd had a chance to live his life to the fullest.

"All Rosa wanted for me to be happy," Carlos said with an honest smile. He turned to gaze at the fake Rosa standing behind him and looking at him expectantly, waiting for him to kill himself. "You are an insult to her memory, demon." The veil cleared from his eyes. He'd faltered for a moment, but he was finally drawn back from the edge by his anchor: his wife.

"You can go now."

The demon slowly wilted away as soon as he'd said it, as did the construct around him. Facing him as soon as everything became clear was Christina, her hands cupping his cheeks while she stared at him with worry.

"Oh, thank God," she said the moment she noticed he was conscious again. "I was so—" Before Christina could finish what she was saying, Carlos held her tightly and kissed her. Without her, he would be dead.

"You saved me," he said after their lips had parted. "I would have been dead if you hadn't intervened."

"Well, I kind of owed you for the number of times you've saved me," she replied with a smile.

"We have to get out of here."

"Are you sure we can do that, Carlos? So far, we've been able to resist whatever's in this house, but something tells me it'll get worse when we leave this room. For starters, that large, dark, silhouette man could be outside."

"Yes, I am sure. It's just in our minds. He patrols out there to make us think we cannot escape. I'm sure the black goo stuff only affects us because we think it will. After the first dump, we were psychologically programmed to expect horrible things from it and fear it, and that gave it even more power."

"I guess you're right, but you know it's still gonna hurt, right?"

"I'm not scared," Carlos said to his wife with a smile, and he really wasn't. They had survived the worst and proven they could individually overcome the forces of this house. Together, they could help each other get past the obstacles no matter what they might be. As far as Carlos knew, the ghosts could not do any real damage to them, only influence them to damage themselves.

"We can do this together. I genuinely believe so; as long as we trust ourselves and one another, we can overcome anything."

Carlos knew that Christina always felt safe with him, and she would trust his judgment.

"All right. Let's do it."

"Okay." They both took deep breaths, counted to three, and Carlos opened the door, but to his surprise, the Silhouette Man wasn't waiting there. He poked out his head cautiously, trying to check if it was a trick, but the coast was clear in the hallway.

"Let's make a run for it while we can," he said to her, and she nodded. They rushed out, but as they ran, the doors to the hall swung open. The Silhouette Man was in the creepy room with the doll, standing right next to it. The doll was seated on the body—or the skeleton, to be specific—of what they assumed had been a person. The other room looked empty and seemed generally brighter, but they didn't care and kept going to the end of the hallway so they could use the stairs.

"Why is no one chasing us?" Christina inquired, sounding a bit confused.

"Don't ask, honey—Just run!" As far as Carlos was concerned, they had to run first and ask questions later. They needed to go as fast as they could so they could leave and get the bloody suitcase. He was not even sure how to use the suitcase to banish the demons. He'd even burned the thing. A part of him believed the suitcase was intact or it would not have that much power. Maybe his assumptions had been way off, and the suitcase had nothing to do with the house. That would mean they were better off running the moment they'd left the house rather than go back into the house. The worst part of it all was that he knew they'd have to still go back into the house and get into the attic so they could put the suitcase back where they'd found it. For some reason, however, Carlos felt as if he was forgetting something. He couldn't quite put his finger on it, but it was important.

"Carlos!" He was so deep in thought; he hadn't noticed that the stairs had completely disappeared. He would have fallen, possibly to his death, if it weren't for Christina, who had called his attention back to the situation at hand. He tried to stop, but he was running so fast that he was bound to fall if it weren't for Christina holding him back.

"Oh, shit. Thanks. That was a close one," he admitted.

Carlos finally knew why the demons hadn't chased them. He and his wife turned to see several ghosts facing them. There was an Army man, a set of twins who looked no more than eleven years old, a woman with messy hair, the skeleton with the doll, the Silhouette Man, and others. The same question that had been in his head all day came to the forefront again: what the hell was happening?

"We have to believe the stairs are actually there," Carlos said to her.

"Wait. What?"

The ghosts walked toward them slowly, making menacing noises.

They had to act fast. It was then or never.

"Yes. We have to take a leap of faith and believe that we are fine and the stairs are there. If we don't, things could get bad really quick."

"I'm not sure—"

"You just have to believe… in you and in me. The stairs are there… the stairs are there." Reciting this was as much for Carlos as it was for Christina.

The Silhouette Man had already opened his mouth to gush out some of his weird mucus at them. Even though they were prepared for it—or they believed they were—he would surely rather not have to go through that again. Even having the slightest doubt was enough to make the goo work. They both had to believe.

"Okay," Christina told him.

"Good. One…"

The ghosts raised their hands, reaching out for them.

"Two… three!"

They each placed a foot on where the stairs were supposed to be, and they fell.

"Fuck!" Carlos swore as he reflexively protected Christina, and they landed hard on the floor. He definitely had some broken ribs… either that or he had broken something else. Carlos already had a head injury, and now his body was messed up. Christina's leg was messed up and looked like it would no longer work.

"I'm sorry, baby. We have to get going and leave this place. We have to get to the door." Carlos dragged himself up and helped her to her feet. She limped a bit, but they knew they had to leave. Carlos did not know what they would do when they got to the suitcase, but one thing was for sure, there was no way he was going back into the building.

The ghouls hovered down, chasing them as they struggled to leave the house. They were both bleeding, but neither cared. It was do or die. Carlos wondered why the ghosts weren't moving any faster. It seemed as if they could appear anywhere they wanted in the house, but now they were moving incredibly slow.

He opened the door, and they went outside. It was evening and almost dark, but they didn't care about that. They went straight for the trash.

Carlos turned back to notice that the beings were stuck in the doorjamb. Why weren't they chasing them? He saw that ghost that had appeared as Rosa right outside of the house and even heard the guitar sounds.

He opened the trashcan and saw that the suitcase was intact. Both of them sighed in relief.

"Oh, thank God," Carlos said, reaching for the suitcase. He opened his eyes. Beside him, Christina also opened her eyes. All they could hear was laughter.

"What… what is happening?" Christina asked. "We were outside and reaching for the trash."

Slowly but surely, it donned on Carlos, who began laughing along with the weird laughter that echoed through the attic.

Yes, they were back in the attic.

"Why are you laughing? This isn't funny?" Christina sounded annoyed. "How did we get here?"

"I can't believe this," Carlos said. "I never went to work this morning. That was why it all felt so familiar. There were fewer people, and the sounds of the guitar were able to reach me at work. It was all so weird because I was in the house all along. This fucking house… the house used my memories of where I used to live and work before to create the fake reality. That was why and how everyone looked familiar or the same."

"What do you mean? I know you left."

"It was all in this house," he explained, still stunned at the fact. "We haven't left the house since we threw that suitcase away. It's been torture nonstop."

"Oh, God," Christina said in disbelief. Everything up until then had been nothing but sinking deeper and deeper into the hellish creation in the haunted house of doom. How the hell would they get out now?

"We were under the house's spell from the very start," he said, resting his head on his palm. "I just can't fucking believe this."

To be continued…

(This story was inspired by an idea from my dear reader Jennifer Williams)

HORRORS NEXT DOOR

Find out what happened to Hernandez family and discover more scary stories in "HORRORS OF THE NIGHT 4"

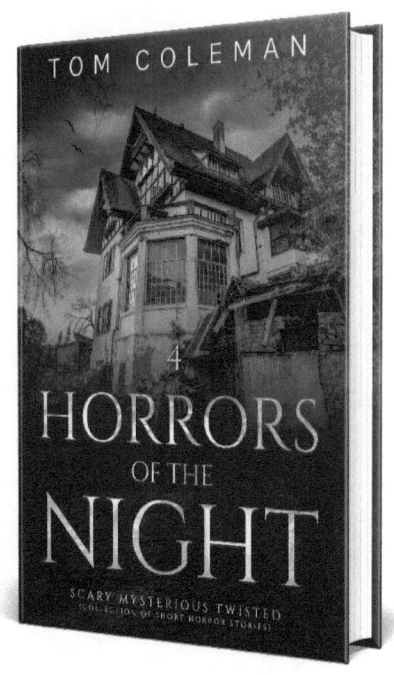

HORRORS NEXT DOOR

152

TOM COLEMAN

We are gathering all people with a passion for Horror and Thrillers in our special group. If you want to be in and connect with us, join our group :)

Join here:

https://www.facebook.com/groups/541739063097831/

HORRORS NEXT DOOR

TOM COLEMAN

HONEST REVIEW REQUEST

Dear reader, if you liked my book and want me to keep on writing, please go online and leave an honest review.

Your review means a lot to me, and it will encourage me to surprise you with more books and stories.

THANK YOU!

www.ingramcontent.com/pod-product-compliance
Lightning Source LLC
LaVergne TN
LVHW040150080526
838202LV00042B/3101